MY 1ST GRAPHIC NOVEL®

FIRST BASE BLUES

STONE ARCH BOOKS
a capstone imprint

My First Graphic Novels are published by Stone Arch Books
A Capstone Imprint
1710 Roe Crest Drive
North Mankato, Minnesota 56003
www.capstonepub.com

Library of Congress Cataloging-in-Publication Data
Yasuda, Anita.
  First base blues / by Anita Yasuda ; illustrated
by Steve Harpster.
     p. cm. — (My first graphic novel)
  Summary: Nico is disappointed when he
does not get to be the shortstop on his baseball
team—will he learn in time that all positions on
a team are important?
  ISBN 978-1-4342-3279-3 (library binding)
  ISBN 978-1-4342-3863-4 (pbk.)
  1. Baseball—Comic books, strips, etc.
2. Baseball stories. 3. Disappointment—Comic
books, strips, etc. 4. Disappointment—Juvenile
fiction. 5. Attitude change—Comic books,
strips, etc. 6. Attitude change—Juvenile fiction.
7. Graphic novels. [1. Graphic novels.
2. Baseball—Fiction.] I. Harpster, Steve, ill.
II. Title. III. Series: My first graphic novel.

  PZ7.7.Y37Fi 2012
  741.5'973—dc23

2011032217

Art Director: Bob Lentz
Graphic Designer: Brann Garvey
Production Specialist: Michelle Biedscheid

Printed in the United States of America in Stevens Point, Wisconsin.
102011   006404WZS12

FIRST BASE
BLUES

written by
Anita Yasuda

illustrated by
Steve Harpster

HOW TO READ A GRAPHIC NOVEL

Graphic novels are easy to read. Boxes called panels show you how to follow the story. Look at the panels from left to right and top to bottom.

Read the word boxes and word balloons from left to right as well. Don't forget the sound and action words in the pictures.

The pictures and the words work together to tell the whole story.

Nico loved the Bears. They were his favorite baseball team.

Nico especially loved Ben Scott. He was the Bears' shortstop.

Nico got to meet Ben once.

Nico wondered if playing baseball was as much fun as watching baseball.

Nico practiced for tryouts with his dad. He was good at some things, but he needed to work on others.

Finally, baseball started. At practice, Nico worked on his hitting. He worked on his throwing.

He chased down every ball.

He wanted to be shortstop, just like his hero.

He carried Ben's baseball card for luck.

But Ben's good luck card did not work.

Nico was stuck playing first base, while his friend, Jen, got to play shortstop.

Jen was very fast, and she had a great arm.

Since Nico wasn't shortstop, he didn't care about baseball anymore. He was late for practices.

He didn't run for the ball or try to hit it.

He juggled his glove when he was on first base.
He picked at the grass.

Coach could see that Nico was no longer working hard. He stopped Nico after practice one day.

After that, Nico came to practice on time.
He worked on his batting.

He was ready to catch the ball when it came his way.

Soon it was opening day. A player from the other team batted first. She hit it high in the air.

The ball bounced before someone could catch it.

The batter made it to first base.

Safe!

The next batter hit the ball. It flew across the field. Jen quickly scooped up the ball.

She threw the ball to Nico at first base.

Nico was ready. He reached with his glove.

He caught the ball. The runner was out!

Nico thought fast. He threw the ball to second.

It was a double play!

Everyone played great! The game ended in a tie.

Nico still loved the Bears.

Ben Scott was still his hero.

And Ben's card was still his good luck charm.

But Nico didn't want to be shortstop anymore.
He was having too much fun playing first base.

BIOGRAPHIES

ANITA YASUDA lives in a small town with her husband, daughter, and dog, Ted. When she is not writing, she enjoys musical theater, Pilates, skiing, and walking Ted. While Ted is happy to just chase squirrels, Anita and her daughter love to travel. They have been on more than 100 trips and hope to visit every continent some day.

STEVE HARPSTER has loved drawing funny cartoons, mean monsters, and goofy gadgets since he was able to pick up a pencil. Now he does it for a living. Steve lives in Columbus, Ohio, with his wonderful wife, Karen, and their sheepdog, Doodle.

GLOSSARY

ATTENTION (uh-TEN-shuhn) — careful listening or watching

FAVORITE (FAY-vuh-rit) — the person or thing that you like best

IMPORTANT (im-PORT-uhnt) — worth taking seriously and can make a big difference

POSITION (puh-ZISH-uhn) — in sports, the place where a person plays

SHORTSTOP (SHORT-stop) — in baseball, the player whose position is between second and third base

DISCUSSION QUESTIONS

1. Nico loves baseball more than anything. What sport or hobby do you love most?

2. In the book, Nico does not want to play first base. What would you do if you had to play a position that you did not like?

3. Nico takes his baseball card everywhere. Have you ever owned something that you took everywhere? If so, what was it? Where did it go?

WRITING PROMPTS

1. If you could meet your sports hero, who would it be? Write a few sentences about him or her.

2. Baseball is exciting. Draw three things you see at a baseball field. Label your picture.

3. In the book, there are sound and action words next to some of the pictures. Pick at least two of those words. Then write your own sentences using those words.

MY FIRST GRAPHIC NOVEL

These books are the perfect introduction to the world of safe, appealing graphic novels. Each story uses familiar topics, repeating patterns, and core vocabulary words appropriate for a beginning reader. Combine the entertaining story with comic book panels, exciting action elements, and bright colors and a safe graphic novel is born.

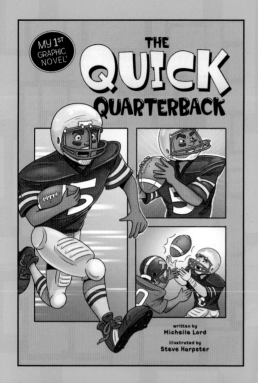

MY 1ST GRAPHIC NOVEL

THE QUICK QUARTERBACK

written by
Michelle Lord

illustrated by
Steve Harpster

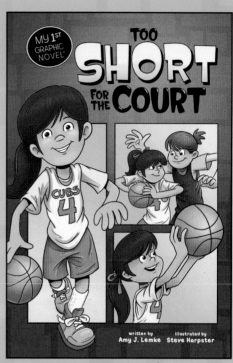

MY 1ST GRAPHIC NOVEL

TOO SHORT FOR THE COURT

written by
Amy J. Lemke

illustrated by
Steve Harpster

MY 1ST GRAPHIC NOVEL

THE SWIM RACE

written by
Anita Yasuda

illustrated by
Steve Harpster

MY 1ST GRAPHIC NOVEL

FIRST BASE BLUES

written by
Anita Yasuda

illustrated by
Steve Harpster